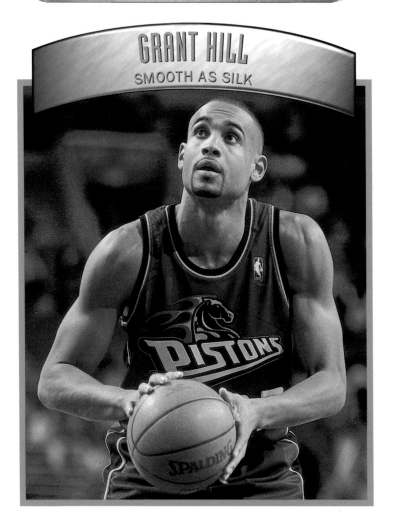

★ SPORTS STARS ★

GRANT HILL
SMOOTH AS SILK

BY MARK STEWART

Children's Press®
A Division of Grolier Publishing
New York London Hong Kong Sydney
Danbury, Connecticut

Photo Credits

Photographs ©: AllSport USA: 31, 45 left (Nathaniel Butler/NBA), 21, 26 (Jonathan Daniel), 12 (Stephen Dunn), 11 (Damian Strohmeyer); AP/Wide World Photos: 6 (Detroit News, Joe DeVera), 22, 23, 32, 34, 45 right; Bob Donnan Photography: 15, 17, 18, 44 left; NBA Photos: 25 (Nathaniel S. Butler), 40 (Scott Cunningham); Rocky Widner: 37, 46, 47; SportsChrome East/West: cover, 3, 28, 43, 44 right (Rich Kane).

Visit Children's Press on the Internet at:
http://publishing.grolier.com

Library of Congress Cataloging-in-Publication Data

Stewart, Mark.
    Grant Hill : smooth as silk / by Mark Stewart.
      p. cm. — (Sports stars)
      Includes index.
      Summary: Examines the career of the star basketball player Grant Hill, from his childhood to his pro career with the Detroit Pistons.
      ISBN 0-516-21219-2 (lib.bdg.)   0-516-26484-2 (pbk.)
      1. Hill, Grant—Juvenile literature. 2. Basketball players—United States—Biography—Juvenile literature. [1. Hill, Grant. 2. Basketball players. 3. Afro-Americans—Biography.] I. Title. II. Series.
GV884.H55S74   1999
796.323'092—dc21
[B]   98–45309
                                    CIP
                                    AC

CONTENTS

★ 1 ★

MAN IN MOTION

Grant Hill brings the ball across midcourt for the Detroit Pistons. At 6'8", he has a clear view of the opposition. As he glides to the right, he watches the defense rotate. His eyes light up when he notices something no one else on the floor can see. In a flash, he takes a step toward his man, changes his dribble quickly from his right hand to his left, and bursts toward the lane. Another defender slides over to stop him, and Grant kicks the ball across the court to a teammate. As the defense scrambles to recover, the ball is lofted high in the air. Grant rises to meet it, grasps it firmly in both hands, then sends it crashing down through the basket.

The opposing coach can only smile and shake his head. How can you teach your players to stop something they do not even know is happening to them? As usual, Grant Hill is thinking two steps ahead of the competition . . . and playing a mile over their heads.

★ 2 ★

CALVIN'S KID

Having a famous dad can be a lot of fun. You get to go places and meet people other kids do not. Grant Hill's dad, Calvin, was a running back for the Cowboys, Redskins, and Browns. At first, Grant loved being "Calvin's kid," but as he got older, his father's notoriety created some problems for him. Everyone Grant met asked him about what it was like to be the son of an NFL star. He could never be sure whether they were interested in him or his father. Also, he was under constant pressure to excel in sports. "I was always expected to be the best athlete because of my father," Grant says. "It didn't matter if I was playing on a team or playing kick the can."

Grant's parents had high expectations for their only child, but football was not part of the plan. They forbade Grant to play football—partly because they knew how rough it was, but mostly to avoid comparisons to Calvin. Instead, Grant played soccer. From soccer he developed balance, quick feet, and an explosive first step that served him well in another sport, basketball. Grant got hooked on hoops when he was 10 years old. He attended a college game with his father and was swept up in the excitement and energy of the event. From that day on, Grant watched all of the live games, highlight shows, and videos he could. Eventually, he began to see how plays develop and how defenses work. This had a big impact on his playing, which improved rapidly.

Grant idolized his father. But soon Calvin was competing with basketball star Julius "Dr. J" Erving for his son's admiration. "I used to watch what he did on TV, and then would try to do on the Nerf basket what he did on a 10-foot basket,"

Calvin and Janet Hill cheer their son during a college game.

Grant remembers. "My role models were my father, Julius Erving, and Arthur Ashe—great men, positive people. I hope people say the same things about me when I'm 40."

Grant's father, Calvin Hill, was an All-Pro NFL running back.

By the time Grant enrolled at Langston Hughes Junior High School in Silver Spring, Maryland, he was starting to distinguish himself as a star athlete in his own right. Still, having his dad around made him uncomfortable. In eighth grade, Calvin came to school one day to talk to the students at a special assembly. Grant pretended he was sick and hid in the nurse's office. On another occasion, when his father picked him up from basketball practice in a Mercedes-Benz, Grant begged him to use the family's old Volkswagen in the future. He did not want the other boys to think he was trying to look better than them. Indeed, Grant seemed happiest when he could just fade into the background. That winter he served as water boy for the South Lakes High School junior varsity basketball team, and he had the time of his life.

The following year, Grant tried out for the South Lakes junior varsity (JV) team. The varsity coach, Wendell Byrd, thought Grant was too good for the JV, and asked him to play for him. He became the first freshman in school history to start for the varsity, and by season's end he was the best player on the squad.

The following season, Grant was voted Northern Virginia Player of the Year—a rare feat for a sophomore. He would earn this honor in his junior and senior years, as well, and he twice led South Lakes to the state semifinals. In 1989, he was invited to attend the famous Five Star Basketball Camp and was named its Most Outstanding Player.

By the fall of 1989, Grant was near the top of every college's recruiting list, with most schools ranking him among the top five high-school forwards. He was polished and versatile on the court, and serious and dedicated in the classroom. Not only was Grant a good student, he even found time to tutor elementary school and junior high students in his spare time. When it came to

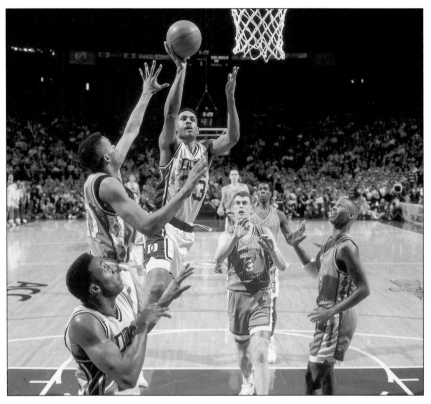

Grant believes his choice to attend Duke University was a sound one. He wanted a great education and a top basketball program.

choose a college, he wanted a great basketball program, a first-rate education, and a short drive home on the holidays. Grant chose Duke University, just a few hours south, in Durham, North Carolina.

★ 3 ★

NOT AFRAID
TO BE GOOD

Duke was the perfect choice. Grant felt comfortable on campus and found his classes both interesting and challenging. He also fit right into the Duke system. Coach Mike Krzyzewski (pronounced shuh-SHEV-skee) emphasized a team concept at both ends of the court. But he also encouraged the Blue Devils to step up and make big plays if they thought they could. Coach Krzyzewski believed Grant was this kind of player, but noticed that he was tentative at times. He pulled his star freshman aside and told him not to be afraid to be good. Grant knew just what he meant. From that moment on, he played with greater authority and confidence, and Duke became a dominant team.

Grant rises to the hoop for an uncontested jam. His play as a freshman helped Duke become a dominant team.

Grant throws down a two-handed dunk.

The stars of the Blue Devils were clutch-shooting center Christian Laettner and playmaking point guard Bobby Hurley. In the 1991 NCAA Tournament, the Blue Devils advanced to the championship game against Kansas University. Grant, who was still a fairly well-kept secret, became a household name with one magnificent play. Streaking down the right side, he elevated in anticipation of an alley-oop pass. The ball, however, was thrown behind him. He reached back with one arm, plucked the errant pass out of the air, and then jackknifed his body in one explosive motion to slam the ball through the hoop. To this day, many consider Grant's dunk to be the most amazing in college history. From that point on, it was all Blue Devils, as Duke won the national title.

Grant's parents were in the stands watching it all. Janet Hill says that Calvin was happier that night than when he won the Super Bowl. Of course, after the game, the ultra-competitive Hill men were up to their old tricks. "I teased him that I won my first championship as a college freshman," laughs Grant, "and it took him a couple of years with the Cowboys to get his." Calvin's response? He reminded Grant that, as good as he was, he only had half the old man's genes. Imagine how good he would be if he had the other half!

Grant continued to improve as a sophomore. During one stretch, Hurley went out with a broken foot and Coach Krzyzewski asked Grant to handle the ball. He did an excellent job. Years of watching videotapes and highlights had paid off. Grant could read the floor beautifully and think two and three passes ahead of the opposition. Hurley returned in time for the NCAA Tournament, and once again the Blue Devils won the title. It marked the first time in 19 years that a school had won back-to-back national championships.

In Grant's junior season, Duke failed to reach the Final Four. Though disappointed, he took great pride in two honors that came his way after

**Grant (left) and his teammates hoist the NCAA
championship trophy for the second consecutive year.**

the season. Grant was recognized as a Second-
Team All-American, and he won the Henry Iba
Corinthian Award as the nation's top defensive
player. Had he chosen to leave Duke and enter
the NBA Draft, some believe Grant would have
been the second or third player chosen. But
closing the book on his Blue Devil career was
never an option. Grant wanted to complete his
college degree and was looking forward to his
senior year—both in class and on the court.

The 1994 Blue Devils needed Grant to step up and take charge, and he led them to the NCAA Finals.

When the 1993–94 season began, Grant was the lone star on a shaky Duke team. Somehow, Duke made it all the way back to the NCAA championship game. Against the University of Arkansas, one of the deepest Final Four teams in

Grant gets the "final snip" as Duke celebrates making the 1994 Final Four by cutting down the net.

memory, the Blue Devils held off wave after wave of Razorback supersubs and clung to a slim lead as the final seconds ticked away. Arkansas's Scotty Thurman threw up a prayer from three-point territory and Grant's roommate, Antonio Lang, barely missed blocking it. Incredibly, the ball went in, and with it went all hopes of a third title for Grant. Despite the obvious disappointment, the Blue Devils' run was heralded as a magnificent accomplishment—both for the school and for Grant.

★ 4 ★

HEIR JORDAN

In the early 1980s, the Detroit Pistons were the doormats of the NBA. The team was able to rebuild quickly thanks to a series of smart draft choices, including guard Isiah Thomas. By the end of the decade, Detroit was on its way to a pair of NBA championships. During this time, the Pistons were one of Grant's favorite teams. Age and injury had caught up to the Pistons, though, and they won just 20 games during the 1993–94 season. Because of their poor finish, the team now held the third selection in the 1994 NBA Draft, after the Milwaukee Bucks and Dallas Mavericks.

Grant shows off his new team colors after being selected by the Detroit Pistons in the 1994 NBA Draft.

Joe Dumars (left) and Grant on the Piston bench.

On draft day, Grant waited anxiously as
the Bucks and Mavs announced their picks.
Milwaukee chose Glenn Robinson of Purdue,
the nation's leading scorer. Next, Dallas claimed
point guard Jason Kidd. "This was one time I
didn't mind finishing third", says Grant, who
was ecstatic when the Pistons called his name.
"Detroit was where I wanted to go, and I crossed
my fingers and said my prayers and ended up
where I wanted to be."

Grant joined a club that planned to rebuild around him over the next few years. Two young guards, Lindsey Hunter and Allan Houston, would be expected to form the nucleus of the club with Grant, while Joe Dumars—the only starter left over from Detroit's glory days— would provide veteran leadership. Grant was immediately taken with Dumars. "He told me he had no ego," he says of his initial meeting with Dumars. "The only thing he wanted to do was win. I couldn't believe that someone who had accomplished as much as he has came to a 21-year-old kid and said this."

The most surprising part of Grant's first season had nothing to do with his experience on the court. Grant came into the league a year after Michael Jordan left basketball to pursue his baseball career. The NBA had plenty of big names remaining—Charles Barkley, David Robinson, and Hakeem Olajuwon, to mention a few—but there were no young players who seemed ready to achieve superstar status.

As a rookie, Grant was touted as the heir to Michael Jordan.

When Grant got off to a hot start, everyone became very excited. He seemed to be the answer to Detroit's problems. Grant was handsome, smart, and polite. He had been a winner at every level, and he expressed himself well. In the eyes of the league and its business partners, Grant was the perfect "good guy" to replace Jordan.

Grant was just a rookie playing for a losing team, yet he was offered several rich endorsement deals. He signed agreements with Sprite, Kellogg's, and GMC Trucks, and Fila named a basketball shoe after him. A national magazine called *Gentlemen's Quarterly* ran a story entitled, "Can Grant Hill Save Sports?"

The fact that he was playing brilliantly only made things crazier. All of the love and admiration that had been showered on Jordan was now heaped upon Grant. When the final balloting was tabulated for the NBA All-Star Game, Grant had more votes than anyone else in the league— something no rookie had ever done before. "I didn't deserve it," he is quick to point out. "It was because of my personality, not my play."

As level-headed as he was, it was difficult for Grant not to get caught up in all the hype, especially when people started calling him "Heir Jordan." Grant did not realize it, but he had begun to act and speak and play in ways that were not always natural to him. Earvin "Magic" Johnson, who knew a thing or two about hype, came up to him and told him he was not the next anyone, he was Grant Hill. "You are not a 40-point man," Johnson said. "You bring other things to the floor, and that's what you should concentrate on developing."

With a few weeks left in the season, Michael Jordan returned to the Chicago Bulls. That took the spotlight off of Grant, and let him put his first season in perspective. The Pistons had made a slight improvement, and probably would have done better had several key players not been injured. Grant finished as the NBA's 20th leading scorer, with 19.9 points per game, and he averaged more minutes per contests than

Despite being a rookie, Grant (right) received more votes than anyone else for the 1995 All-Star Game.

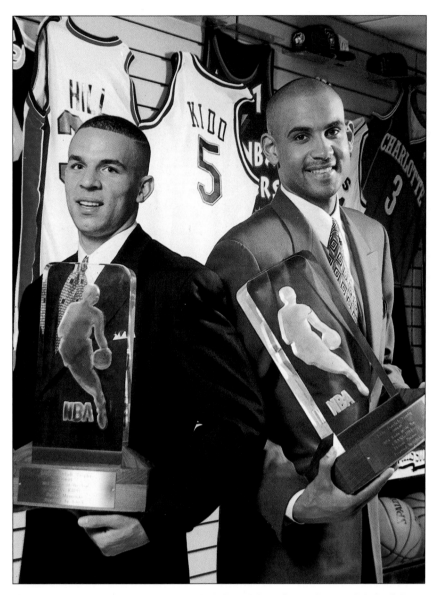

**Grant shared the 1994–95 NBA Rookie of the Year title with
Dallas Maverick Jason Kidd (left).**

all but seven other players. At the end of the year, he and Jason Kidd finished in a tie for the Rookie of the Year award.

The 1995–96 season began with great excitement in Detroit. New coach Doug Collins was starting his first season with the team, and the Pistons had picked up power forward Otis Thorpe over the summer. In Grant's first year, the team was merely expected to try. In his second, the fans wanted to make the playoffs. Coach Collins knew that would depend on Grant's development, and he pushed his young star all season long. Coach Collins urged him to play smarter, be a leader, and to take charge when the team was flat.

Thanks to Grant's leadership and the hot shooting of Allan Houston, the Pistons finished 46–36 and made the playoffs. In the first round, they faced Shaquille O'Neal and the Orlando Magic, who finished the year with 60 wins. Orlando swept the series, winning the first two games easily and pulling out a three-point win in the final contest.

Grant goes to the hoop during the 1996 Olympics.

Charles Barkley (left) and Grant share a laugh after Team USA receives its gold medals.

The summer of 1996 found Grant in Atlanta, Georgia, as a member of the United States national team competing in the Olympics. His teammates included Jordan and Scottie Pippen, the two players he most admired. Grant took advantage of his time with the team by observing these players and analyzing their games. To become the best, he explains, you must learn from those that are the best. The most important lesson Grant learned was that, as hard as they worked in practice and during games, players like Jordan and Pippen always seemed to be having fun. The U.S. "Dream Team" destroyed the competition, and Grant played very well. He left Atlanta with a prized possession: an Olympic gold medal.

★ 5 ★

UPS AND DOWNS

Grant began his third year in the pros with a positive outlook and high hopes of finishing right up there with Scottie and Michael in the Central Division standings. The Detroit fans were not as confident. The team had let Allan Houston sign with the New York Knicks, which meant that the bulk of the outside scoring duties would fall to aging Joe Dumars. There were also questions at center and point guard. If the Pistons hoped to go anywhere, they would be counting more than ever on Grant.

Grant responded to this pressure magnificently. Over the first half of the season, he was, without a doubt, the most valuable player in the league. He ranked among the NBA leaders in points, rebounds, assists, shooting percentage, and steals.

Coach Doug Collins gives Grant instructions during a break in play.

Grant also was taking the ball to the basket with much more authority, forcing teams to foul him. At first, the referees did not call many of these fouls. But Grant demanded, and eventually earned, their attention and respect.

The Pistons were playing well behind Grant, too. Dumars shot well, centers Terry Mills and Theo Ratliff created matchup problems for opponents, and Hunter and Thorpe also were consistent contributors. The Pistons finished 54–28 and committed the fewest turnovers in league history. As for Grant, he had a blast. He took his own advice and enjoyed the season. He was the only player in the NBA to lead his team in scoring, rebounds, and assists, and he topped the NBA in triple-doubles.

There were signs, however, that all was not well. The Pistons had built a remarkable 20–4 mark early in the season, but failed to win consistently after that. Mills was a great outside-shooting center and Ratliff was a monster inside, yet neither developed the all-around game teams

need from their pivotmen in the playoffs.
And Dumars, whose three-point shooting
was spectacular in November and December,
looked worn out by April. In the first round of
the playoffs, Detroit tangled with the Atlanta
Hawks in a hard-fought five-game series. Detroit
grabbed a 2–1 lead and had a chance to wrap it
up at home, but Atlanta's front line of Dikembe
Mutombo, Ty Corbin, and Christian Laettner
overwhelmed the Pistons and led Atlanta to
victory in Games Four and Five. Once again,
Detroit had failed to advance beyond the
first round.

Grant was beginning to realize something
about life as a professional athlete. No matter
how hard you work to improve yourself,
sometimes there is little you can do to improve
your surroundings. Grant had become one of the
best players in the NBA, but the Pistons, despite
their good record, did not appear to be building a
winning club. They relied on Grant's versatility
so much that they were becoming a one-man

When in doubt, Detroit usually gives the ball to Grant and lets him do his thing.

--- ★ ★ ★ ---

team. And those teams never win championships. The Detroit defense ground to a halt, and the losses began to pile up. The Pistons ended up missing the playoffs for the first time since Grant's rookie year.

Grant tried to remain upbeat and take something positive from this lost season. That is what great players do. He took a hard look at his own game, and decided that there was still some room for improvement. The team's great failing had been its lack of outside shooting. Grant vowed to improve this part of his repertoire, so that players would be forced to guard him beyond 20 feet. He also promised himself to concentrate harder on defense and rebounding, although he already ranks among the league's best small forwards in these areas. "I want to get to the point where at both ends of the court I put fear in somebody's heart," he says.

Grant also took a hard look at himself and decided that he was devoting too much energy to always being a good guy. Somewhere along the way, he had gotten caught up in his own publicity. Grant was afraid to speak his mind or lose his cool, keeping his emotions bottled up inside. From now on, he is just going to be himself. "So much has been made of me just being some sort of perfect person, and anyone that knows me knows that I'm not perfect," he says. "I'm real, just like everybody else. I don't have to go out of my way to be a nice guy. I think I'm *already* a nice guy! That is hardly a secret around the NBA."

On the court, Grant gets scarier each season. There are only one or two defenders in the NBA who can guard him one-on-one, and should he develop a consistent three-pointer, he could average 30 or more per game. He is already the league's best ball-handling forward, and he is a big-play defender who can turn a game around with a key steal or dramatic block.

That is why, regardless of his team's record, Grant Hill is regarded as one of the NBA's biggest winners.

Grant has a message for his NBA opponents: "No More Mr. Nice Guy!"

C ★ H ★ R ★ O ★ N

1972 • October 5: Grant is born in Dallas, Texas.

1987 • Grant was named Northern Virginia Player of the Year as a sophomore at South Lakes High School.

1989 • Grant attends the Five Star Basketball Camp and is named its Most Outstanding Player.

1990 • Grant enters Duke University

1991 • The Duke Blue Devils win the NCAA championship against Kansas University.

1992 • The Blue Devils win their second straight NCAA title—the first time in 19 years that a school has won back-to-back national championships.

1994 • Grant is selected third overall in the NBA Draft by his favorite team, the Detroit Pistons.

1995 • Grant receives more votes than anyone else in the league for the All-Star Game—a first for an NBA rookie.

O ★ L ★ O ★ G ★ Y

- Grant ties with Jason Kidd for NBA Rookie of the Year honors.

1996
- For the second consecutive year, Grant receives the most votes for the NBA All-Star Game.

- Grant competes as a member of the United States national team at the Olympics in Atlanta, Georgia and brings home a gold medal.

1997–98
- Grant records his third straight 20-point season.

1998–99
- Grant is the only Piston to start all 50 of the team's games.

- Grant is named second-team All-NBA.

1999–00
- Grant has career highs in scoring with 25.8, free throw percentage with .795, and three point percentage with .347.

- Grants signs with the Orlando Magic in the off-season.

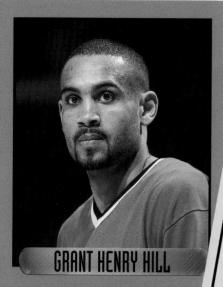

GRANT HENRY HILL

GRANT HENRY HILL

Date of Birth **October 5, 1972**
Place of Birth **Dallas, Texas**
Height **6′ 8″**
Weight **225 pounds**
College **Duke University**
Championships **Two-Time NCAA Champion**
Awards 1994 **First-Team All-American**
1994 **ACC Player of the Year**
1995 **NBA Co-Rookie of the Year**
1996 **Olympic Gold Medalist**
1997 **First-Team All-NBA**
1998, 1999 **Second-Team All-NBA**

NBA STATISTICS

Year	Team	Assists per Game	Rebounds per Game	Points per Game
1994–95	Detroit Pistons	5.0	6.4	19.9
1995–96	Detroit Pistons	6.9	9.8	20.2
1996–97	Detroit Pistons	7.3	9.0	21.4
1997–98	Detroit Pistons	6.8	7.7	21.1
1998–99	Detroit Pistons	6.0	7.1	21.1
1999–00	Detroit Pistons	5.2	6.6	25.8
Totals		6.3	7.9	21.6

ABOUT THE AUTHOR

Mark Stewart grew up in New York City in the 1960s and 1970s—when the Mets, Jets, and Knicks all had championship teams. As a child, Mark read everything about sports he could lay his hands on. Today, he is one of the busiest sportswriters around. Since 1990, he has written close to 500 sports stories for kids, including profiles on more than 200 athletes, past and present. A graduate of Duke University, Mark served as senior editor of *Racquet,* a national tennis magazine, and was managing editor of *Super News*, a sporting-goods industry newspaper. His syndicated newspaper column, *Mark My Words*, is read by sports fans nationwide. He is the author of every Grolier All-Pro Biography and 17 titles in the Children's Press Sports Stars series.